VOLTRON
LEGENDARY DEFENDER

Pidge's Story

By Natalie Shaw

Illustrated by Patrick Spaziante

Ready-to-Read

Simon Spotlight

New York   London   Toronto   Sydney   New Delhi

SIMON SPOTLIGHT
An imprint of Simon & Schuster Children's Publishing Division
1230 Avenue of the Americas, New York, New York 10020
This Simon Spotlight edition May 2018
Manufactured in the United States of America 0318 LAK
2 4 6 8 10 9 7 5 3 1
ISBN 978-1-5344-1512-6 (hc)
ISBN 978-1-5344-1511-9 (pbk)
ISBN 978-1-5344-1513-3 (eBook)

Hi. My name is Pidge.
Well, actually, it used to be Katie.
Not too long ago, I was just your
average computer genius.
Now I fly an alien spaceship!

The spaceship that I fly
is called the Green Lion.
It combines with four other lions to
form a super-robot called Voltron.

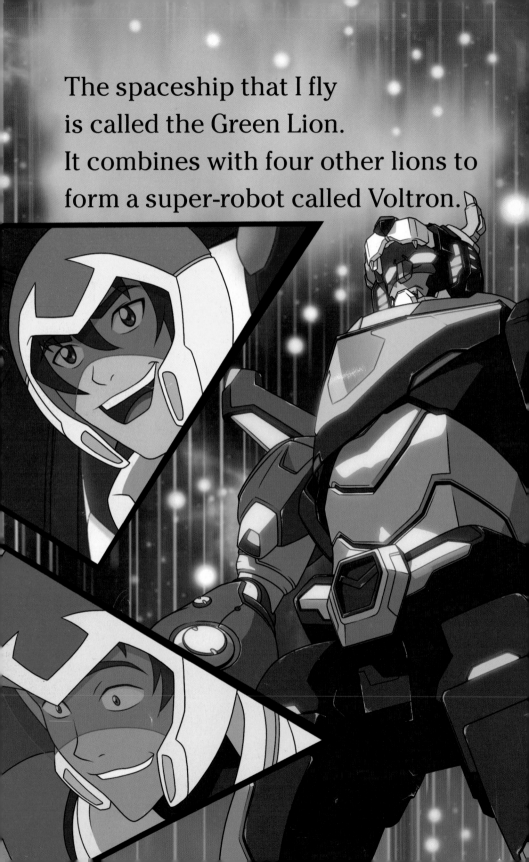

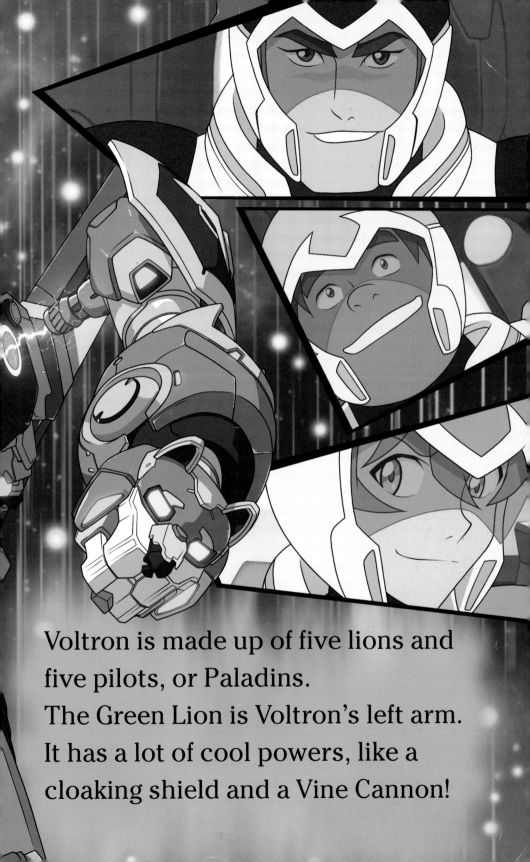

Voltron is made up of five lions and five pilots, or Paladins.
The Green Lion is Voltron's left arm. It has a lot of cool powers, like a cloaking shield and a Vine Cannon!

Before I was a Paladin of Voltron,
I was a girl called Katie.

Back then, I was bullied a lot.
The other kids at school
stole my dessert
and called me names.

Thankfully, my brother Matt knew
how to cheer me up.
Matt was my hero.
He taught me how to crack codes.
He was so smart that
he got into a school
called the Galaxy Garrison!

After Matt graduated, he and my
dad were selected to go on an
important mission to Kerberos,
one of Pluto's moons.
Their pilot, Shiro, was
a legend around our house.

But after landing on Kerberos,
their spaceship stopped
sending signals.
Everyone thought they were gone.

I didn't believe it.
I needed to find out
what really happened.
I snuck into the Garrison
and used their computers.

Did I mention I love computers?
I also like peanut butter cookies,
but I hate peanuts . . .
in case you were wondering!

On the Garrison computer,
I found no evidence of a crash.
My father and brother
might still be safe!

Unfortunately, a guard caught me using the computer.
I was banned from the Garrison forever.

I needed to find more information,
but as Katie, I lost all access.
So I pretended to be a boy and
changed my name to Pidge.
It was a nickname that Matt
used to call me.

As Pidge, I cut my hair and started wearing glasses. The glasses had been a gift from Matt too.

My plan worked!
I became a student
at the Galaxy Garrison.

One night at the Garrison,
I heard a distress alarm.
An alien spaceship crashed nearby!
Shiro, the pilot, was on board.
I hoped that my father and brother
were on board too,
but Shiro was alone.

My classmates Hunk and Lance
and I went to rescue him.
So did Keith, one of Shiro's friends.
Shiro said he had been captured by
aliens who were looking for
something called Voltron.
Sadly, he couldn't remember
much else.

Seeing Shiro gave me hope
of finding my family.

Then the five of us discovered
the Blue Lion on Earth.
Before we knew what was
happening, it took us into space!

I was amazed.
The lion was fast.
It had taken my dad and brother
months to reach Kerberos,
but we passed it in minutes!

The Blue Lion brought us to
a faraway planet called Arus.
There, we met Princess Allura,
who believed I was the
perfect pilot for the Green Lion.

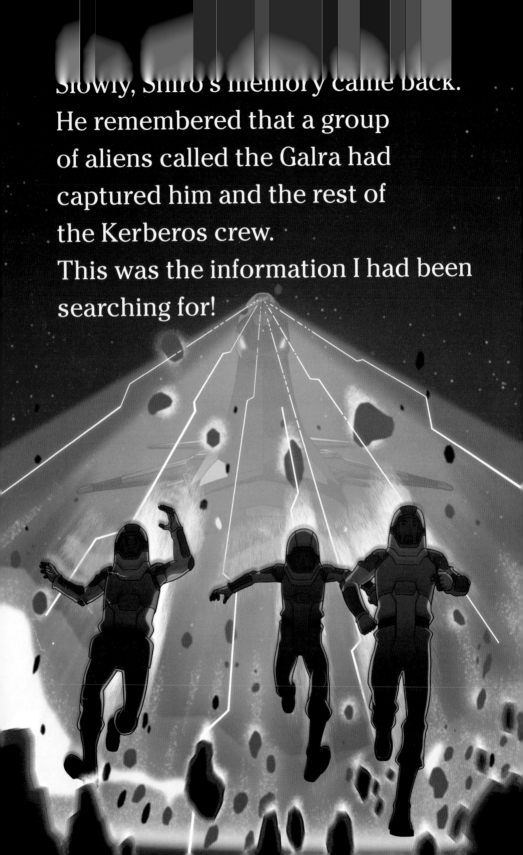

Slowly, Shiro's memory came back. He remembered that a group of aliens called the Galra had captured him and the rest of the Kerberos crew.

This was the information I had been searching for!

I wanted to leave Arus
and find my dad and brother,
but I didn't. You see,
Voltron defends the universe.
As one of its pilots, that means
I defend the universe.
Plus, the team wouldn't have
survived two seconds without
my computer skills.

It wasn't long before
I learned that Matt had escaped
the Galra and faked his own death.

On Matt's fake tombstone, he left a message in a secret code, just like the ones he taught me! I used the code to track down a secret location.

When I got to the secret location,
I saw a masked man.
But then the mask fell off.
It was Matt!

"I can't believe you found me,"
Matt said, after he recognized
me with my new look.
"The thought of you and
Dad kept me going," I told him.

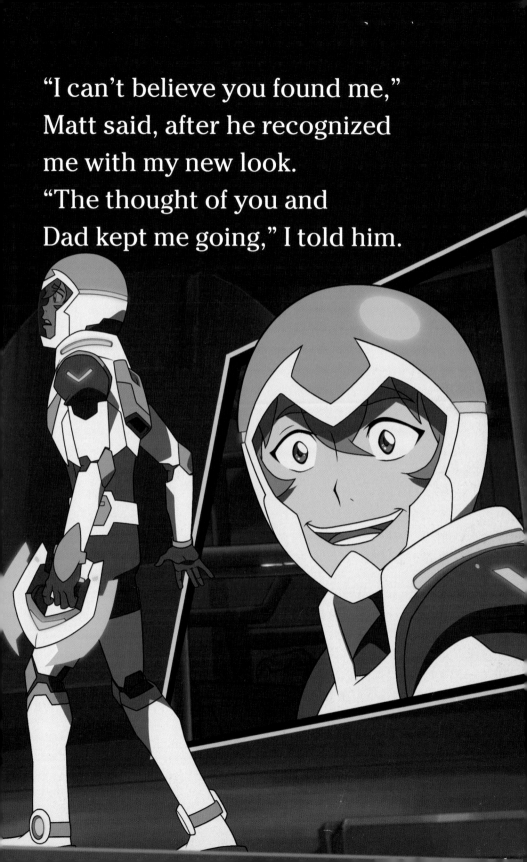

Not long after, we found my dad!
Zarkon, the emperor of the Galra,
had him. We rescued my dad
and he returned to Earth.

One day I hope I return
to Earth too.
But I have a lot more work to do
before that happens,
like saving the universe.

When I lose hope,
I think of something
my dad used to say.
"If you get too worried about what
could go wrong, you might miss
a chance to do something great!"